Ed and Kip

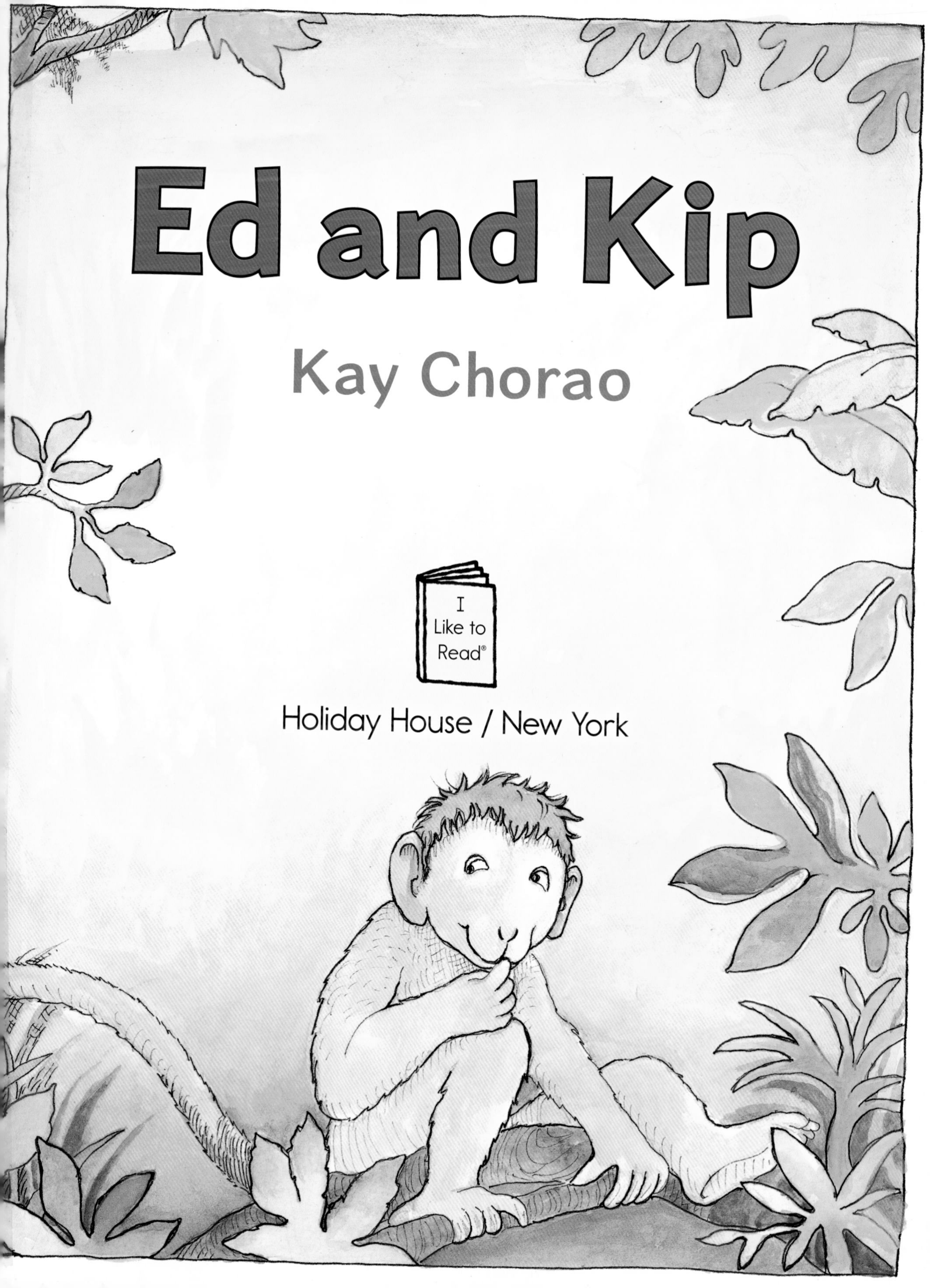

Ed and Kip

Kay Chorao

I Like to Read®

Holiday House / New York

For Sadie, who has been known to play with bugs

I LIKE TO READ is a registered trademark of Holiday House, Inc.

HOLIDAY HOUSE is registered in the U.S. Patent and Trademark Office.
Printed and Bound in October 2014 at Tien Wah Press, Johor Bahru, Johor, Malaysia.
The text typeface is Report School.
The artwork was created with watercolor, gouache, and ink on 140 lb. hot press watercolor paper.
www.holidayhouse.com
3 5 7 9 10 8 6 4 2

Library of Congress Cataloging-in-Publication Data
Chorao, Kay.
Ed and Kip / Kay Chorao. — First edition.
pages cm. — (I like to read)
Summary: Elephants Ed and Kip play with a rolling rock.
ISBN 978-0-8234-2903-5 (hardcover)
[1. Elephants—Fiction. 2. Play—Fiction. 3. Rocks—Fiction. 4. Jungle animals—Fiction.] I. Title.
PZ7.C4463Ed 2014
[E]—dc23
2012045920

ISBN 978-0-8234-3398-8 (paperback)

Monkey dropped a rock.

Ed rolled it to Kip.

Kip rolled it to E
Ouch!
Ed kicked the roc

It rolled into a cave.
Uh-oh.

It rolled out.

A big, big bug came out.
I was taking a nap.
He was mad.

Ed rolled the rock to Bug.

Bug rolled it back.
It rolled far.

It rolled into the water.
Oh.
Oh.
No.

Splash!

Ed and Kip slid down.

They went in the water.

A big head came up.

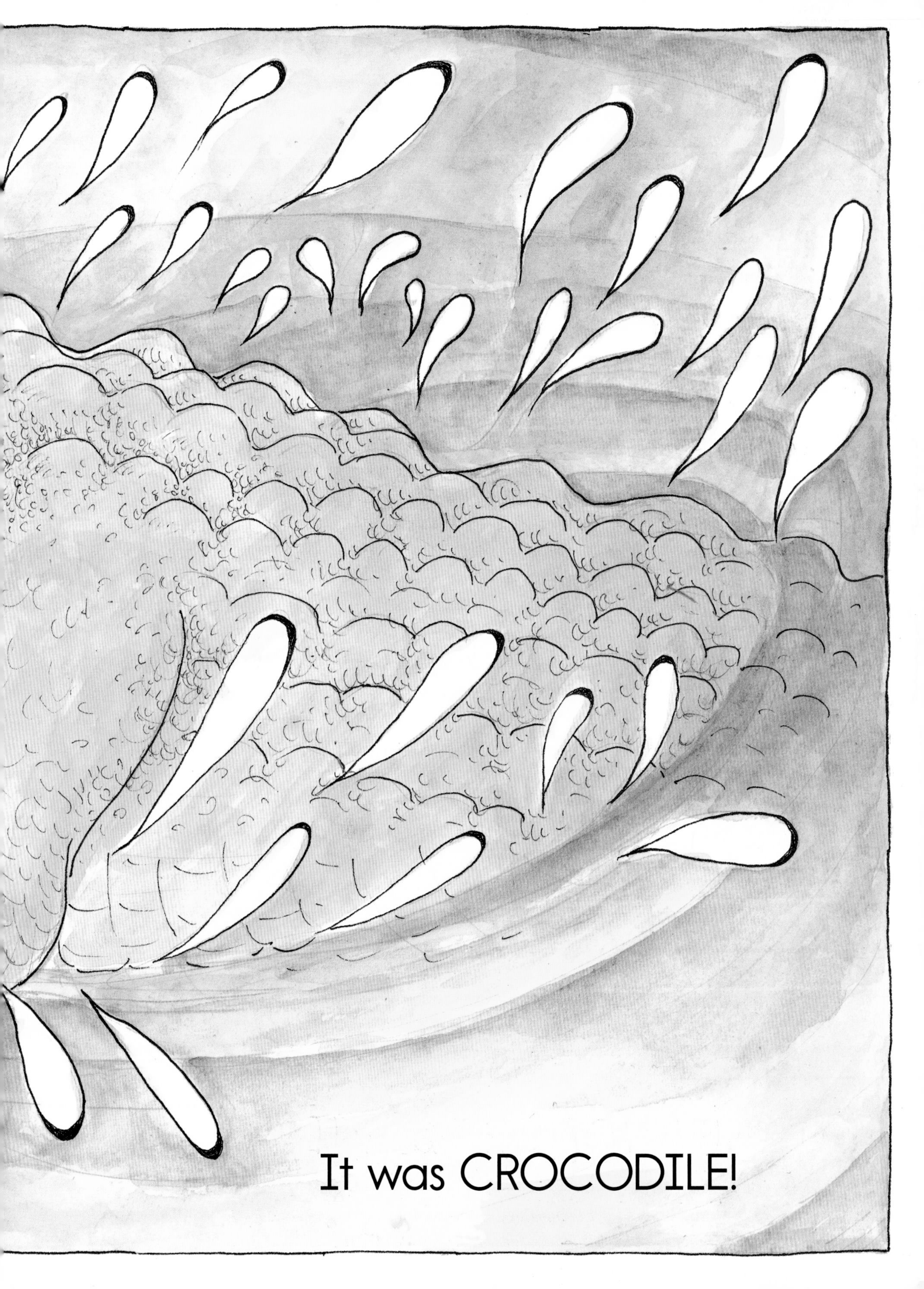

It was CROCODILE!

Ed and Kip were scared.

Crocodile opened wide.

In jumped
Bug.

He poked.

He bit.

Crocodile was surprised.

Bug jumped out.

Crocodile watched Bug.

Ed and Kip threw in the rock.

Crocodile bit hard.
CRUNCH!
Ooooowwwww!

Ed and Kip ran home.
Bug rode.

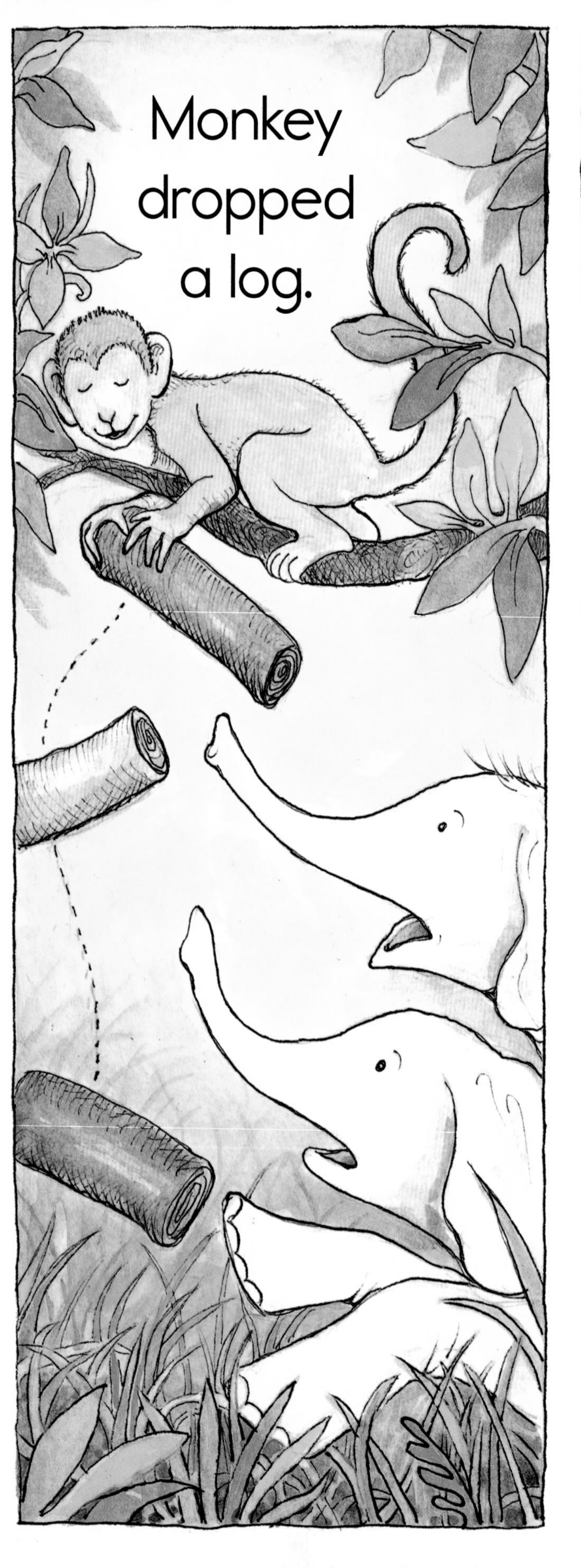
Monkey dropped a log.

MORE FUN!
Back to my nap.

I Like to Read® Books in Paperback
You will like all of them!

Bad Dog by David McPhail
The Big Fib by Tim Hamilton
Boy, Bird, and Dog by David McPhail
Can You See Me? by Ted Lewin
Car Goes Far by Michael Garland
Come Back, Ben by Ann Hassett and John Hassett
The Cowboy by Hildegard Müller
Dinosaurs Don't, Dinosaurs Do by Steve Björkman
Ed and Kip by Kay Chorao
The End of the Rainbow by Liza Donnelly
Fireman Fred by Lynn Rowe Reed
Fish Had a Wish by Michael Garland
The Fly Flew In by David Catrow
Good Night, Knight by Betsy Lewin
Grace by Kate Parkinson
Happy Cat by Steve Henry
I Have a Garden by Bob Barner
I Said, "Bed!" by Bruce Degen
I Will Try by Marilyn Janovitz
Late Nate in a Race by Emily Arnold McCully
The Lion and the Mice by Rebecca Emberley and Ed Emberley
Little Ducks Go by Emily Arnold McCully
Look! by Ted Lewin
Look Out, Mouse! by Steve Björkman
Me Too! by Valeri Gorbachev
Mice on Ice by Rebecca Emberley and Ed Emberley
Pete Won't Eat by Emily Arnold McCully
Pig Has a Plan by Ethan Long
Ping Wants to Play by Adam Gudeon
Sam and the Big Kids by Emily Arnold McCully
See Me Dig by Paul Meisel
See Me Run by Paul Meisel
A Theodor Seuss Geisel Award Honor Book
Sick Day by David McPhail
3, 2, 1, Go! by Emily Arnold McCully
What Am I? Where Am I? by Ted Lewin
You Can Do It! by Betsy Lewin